The Adventures of
SleepyMan

Written by Simone A. Nash

Illustrated by Deborah Smith

Simone Nash

Copyright © 2018 by Simone A. Nash

Edited by Tenita Johnson
So It Is Written, LLC.

Published by EA Books Publishing a division of
Living Parables of Central Florida, Inc. a 501c3
EABooksPublishing.com

ISBN: 1945975792
ISBN-13: 978-1945975790

The Adventures of SleepyMan

DEDICATION

I dedicate this book to my son, Malachi.

Jeremiah 29:11 *For I know the plans I have for you," declares the Lord, "plans to prosper you and not to harm you, plans to give you a hope and a future.*

Once upon a time, there was a little boy named Malcolm.

He was so full of energy!

He would run, jump and swing from early morning until noon.
This was his daily routine.

Mom prepared lunch and called Malcolm to eat.
"Come on, Malcolm! It's time to eat."

After lunch, it was nap time.
This is where trouble started.

Malcolm would fuss and cry because he didn't want to go to sleep. "I'm not sleepy!"

Mom said, "Come and take your nap, son.
When you awake, you will be a little taller and a little stronger."

Malcolm said, "I don't want to be taller or stronger."
He rubbed his eyes.

Mom told him a little story about The Adventures of Sleepy Man. Sleepy Man flew from house to house at noon for nap and at night for bedtime. He came in like a gentle breeze with his large butterfly wings. He took those wings and wrapped them around little children.

Sleepy Man was so gentle that you couldn't feel him, but you knew he was there because the child would begin to rub his or her eyes over and over, becoming very sleepy and irritable.

Malcolm suddenly sat up in the bed, still half asleep, and said,
"Mom, what does irritable mean?"

"This word simply means to get upset," she told him.

Malcolm lay back down and his mom rubbed his head.
She picked up the story where she left off.

"Sleepy Man was very patient and he would not leave
until his mission was complete."

Malcolm, who was now very sleepy, said, "Mission?"
"Yes, his special project. This is his reason for coming."

Before Mom could finish, Malcolm was fast asleep.

When Malcolm awoke from his nap, he asked,
"Mom, am I taller?"
"Yes you are!"
"Am I stronger?"

Malcolm showed his strength by picking up an object in his room.

His mom always clapped her hands and gave Malcolm a big hug and kiss. Malcolm would then jump up and continue playing.

One day Malcolm asked his mom, "Who is Sleepy Man?"
Chuckling, Mom said, "When I was a little girl, my mom told me this
story at bedtime of how the Sleepy Man flew from the north, south,
east and west to all of the houses that had little children.
He flew in like a gentle breeze and comforted those
who had a hard time falling asleep."

Malcom looked puzzled and said, "Mom, did you ever see him?"
She said, "No. But I always had a picture of him in my mind."
"Is he an angel?"
Mom replied, "I believe he is."
"Let's draw a picture of him, Mom!"

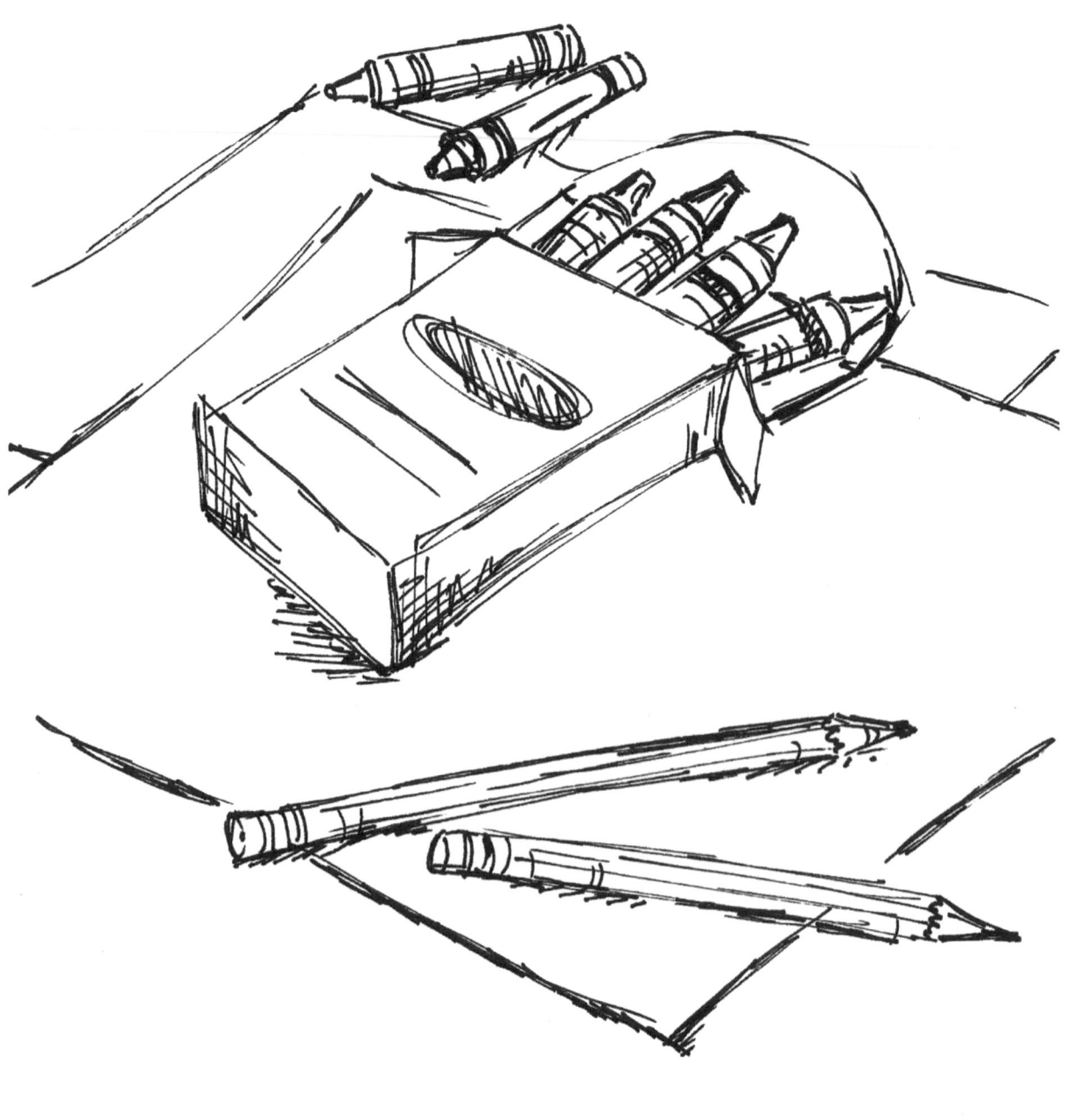

Mom and Malcolm got paper, pencils and crayons to draw.

As they began, Mom told Malcolm, "This was a great idea." Malcolm smiled and continued to draw. Mom told Malcolm to use his imagination.

Then he asked, "What's imagination?"
Mom said, "It is to have an idea in your mind,
like a picture of what you think something should look like."
"Oh, okay!" Malcolm finished drawing.

Malcolm said, "Look, Mom!"

She said, "Great picture, Malcolm! That looks just like the story.
You just might be a future artist!"
Praising Malcolm for his accomplishments
was always important to Mom.

Then, Malcolm jumped up and asked, "Can I go outside to play?"
"Yes," Mom agreed.
Malcolm stopped, turned around and asked,
"Will Sleepy Man come back?"
Mom chuckled. "Yes he will. Have fun son!"

ABOUT THE AUTHOR

Simone A. Nash, a wife of 20 years, a mother of one son and two bonus daughters. Simone is a Business owner, a Certified Chaplain and writer with many imaginative story's to follow. This book was inspired by her Son's humorous antics while he was a child.

ABOUT THE ILLUSTRATOR

Deborah's love for art was nurtured at a young age and has developed into an award winning internationally sold artist. Her focus is to honor God through her art. She has taken her love for Christ and her passion for art and incorporated them into her life's work as an illustrator, painter, sculptor, muralist, and teacher.

Prior to her current enthrallment for book illustrating, she had a distinguished and prestigious career as a Disney Artist, Designer, and Art Director. Deborah resides in Orlando, Florida with her husband.

"It truly is a blessing to pursue and share my passion for art. I will never tire of the joy and fulfillment it brings."

www.3-deborah-smith.artistwebsites.com

www.ingramcontent.com/pod-product-compliance
Lightning Source LLC
Chambersburg PA
CBHW041006170626
46815CB00002B/178